Shining Star

The **My Magical Pony** series:

1: Shining Star
2: Silver Mist
3: Bright Eyes
4: Midnight Snow

Other series by Jenny Oldfield:

Definitely Daisy
Totally Tom
The Wilde Family
Horses of Half Moon Ranch
My Little Life
Home Farm Twins

Shining Star

By Jenny Oldfield

Illustrated by Alasdair Bright

A division of Hodder Headline Limited

First published in Great Britain in 2005
by Hodder Children's Books

3

A Catalogue record for this book is available from the British Library

ISBN 0 340 90323 6
ISBN 978 0 340 90323 0

Printed and bound in Great Britain by Bookmarque Ltd, Croydon, Surrey

The paper and board used in this paperback by Hodder Children's Books are natural recyclable products made from wood grown in sustainable forests. The manufacturing processes conform to the environmental regulations of the country of origin.

Hodder Children's Books
A division of Hodder Headline Limited
338 Euston Road, London NW1 3BH

For Rachel Wade – a star in her own right

Chapter One

Krista stood on the magic spot.

She hadn't known it was magic until the day that it happened, and Shining Star appeared.

"Don't go far," her mum had said. "Supper's almost ready."

Krista had dashed out of the house, on to the cliff path, to stand on the highest point, looking down on Whitton Bay.

She could feel the wind whirling around her, tugging at her jacket. She watched the gulls soar overhead then dip down towards the beach, and the white waves crashing on to the shore.

At first she thought it was birds' wings beating hard against the wind. But the sound was louder, heavier, and it drew close to where Krista stood.

Better get back, she said to herself, *before Mum gets worried.*

But somehow the magic in the air held her. She gazed up at the swirl of grey clouds overhead.

There was a sparkle of silver amongst the grey, like glitter falling from the sky, and the wings beat even louder. The clouds seemed to part.

Krista gasped. She felt dizzy and in danger of falling over the edge of the cliff, way down into the waves.

Through the clouds a ghostly silver shape appeared. The glittering mist drifted towards Krista, there were dark eyes watching her, a pony with a long, silvery mane and wonderful white wings, hovering close by. "Don't be afraid," he said.

Krista had always believed in magic.

"You live in a dream world," her dad would say with a laugh.

"She's animal-mad," her mum would tell everyone. "Especially horses."

"Ponies!" Krista would insist. She couldn't have one of her own yet, not until she was a year or two older, so she helped out at Hartfell stable yard instead. She spent all her spare time there, living and breathing beautiful, proud, wonderful ponies.

"Don't be afraid," the flying pony said.

He hovered above the ground in a glittering mist, the wind ruffling his wing feathers, his dark eyes gazing into Krista's. His mane shone pure silver, his white coat was dusted with a soft sparkle.

"I am Shining Star."

"My name is Krista," she replied.

The pony bent his head closer. "I know. I know everything about you," he whispered.

"Everything?"

He nodded. "I chose you."

"You did?"

"Yes, to help children in trouble."

"But I have to go now," she explained, feeling a bit scared and thinking of home.

Shining Star tossed his head. Silver dust rose in a cloud above him. "I said, don't be afraid."

"I'm not!" Krista replied. Her head buzzed with questions. *Who has chosen me? Who needs help? Where did you come from?*

"Then climb on my back," the pony insisted, alighting on the ground, his wings outstretched. "Come with me."

Come where? she wanted to ask. But instead she took hold of Shining Star's mane and sat astride his broad back. She breathed in a soft, shimmering mist of silver.

"Hold tight," the pony warned.

Then the wind grew even stronger. Shining Star beat his wings and leaped from the cliff path into mid air. Krista's head spun as the rock fell away and they entered what seemed to be a tunnel of whirling grass, sea and sky. They went spinning into darkness as she threw herself forward to clasp the pony's strong neck, then out into a dawn of glittering, silvery blue light.

"We're flying!" she breathed.

High over her world. Below was Whitton Bay – a giant U-shape of rock and golden sand – and the moorlands of Hartfell, and beyond that a thin finger of land called Black Point, where the rock ran into the sea.

His wings beating the air, Shining Star took them higher and higher. Then he turned away from Black Point and soared back towards the bay.

"There's my house!" Krista cried. High Point Farm looked like a tiny grey box on a pale purple slope.

Shining Star swooped low until she could make out their car in the yard and the track leading down the heather hillside to the road. There was someone in the yard, walking from the car into the house.

"There's Dad!" she gasped. "Dad, look up!"

But he didn't hear, and the pony swept on. He took Krista back to the magic spot.

"Well?" he asked, as she let go of his neck and slid to the ground at the highest point on the cliff path.

"Oh!" was all Krista could say. Her eyes glistened with wonder. "Oh! I mean, wow!"

Shining Star raised a front hoof and pawed the ground. "Flying is fun, but it is our job to help," he reminded her.

Still dizzy from flying, Krista nodded. And now the questions came tumbling out. "When? Who? What do you want me to do?"

But the magical pony was getting ready to leave. The silver mist was swirling around him, hiding his face. "Be patient, and the time will soon come," was all he said.

And then he rose into the air, trailing a cloud of glitter.

Krista cried after him. "Tell me what to do!"

But Shining Star was gone. Wings beat steadily, the mist thickened and grey clouds swallowed him.

Chapter Two

"The wind really got up," Krista's dad said over supper. "I was almost blown off my feet out there in the yard."

Krista ate her macaroni cheese and said nothing.

"They said on local radio that it reached gale force," her mum went on. "Oh, and Krista, I heard from Jo at the stables that she needs you early tomorrow morning."

"What time?" For some reason, Krista was keeping quiet about her magical meeting on the cliff path with Shining Star. It was private, like a secret she was bound to keep without actually swearing it.

"Eight o'clock."

"That's cool," she said through her last mouthful of macaroni.

"Don't talk ..." her dad began.

"... With your mouth full!" her mum finished, then laughed.

"Can I feed Spike the leftovers?" Krista asked with a grin.

And she fled outside with the scrapings from the dish, to the nest-box she'd made for her tame hedgehog. She crouched down and tapped the dish with a spoon. "Here, Spike!" she coaxed.

A snuffling and shuffling through the dried

grass and leaves told her that Spike was nearby. Then a dark, pointed snout emerged from the bushes and round black eyes twinkled. "Hey, Spike!" Krista said.

The little hedgehog ambled up to the dish and tucked in.

"Guess what – today I went flying," she confided quietly, "on a silver horse."

Chomp-chomp! Spike guzzled on.

"I did, honest!" Krista looked up at the sky. Light was beginning to fade. There was a red glow over the sea. "But don't tell anyone!"

Chomp-slurp! The hedgehog finished his supper.

"It was …" For a moment, Krista was lost for words. "Well, it was …magical!"

Krista was up early next morning and by half past seven she was cycling over to Hartfell stable yard.

By eight o'clock she was mucking out Shandy, the first of twelve ponies kept on the yard by Jo Weston, who also gave lessons and led trail rides along the cliffs, down on to the beach.

"Thanks for coming at the crack of dawn," Jo told Krista, working in the stable next door. "I'm taking out a ride at ten, and I've got a lesson with Nathan Steele before then."

Krista heaped her barrow high with straw and muck, wheeled it out into the yard, then untied Shandy and led her back into the stable. "Good girl," she breathed, taking off the patient pony's headcollar.

Shandy was a dark bay with a thick black mane and tail.

Next door, Jo was picking out the feet of a new chestnut gelding called Drifter – a three-year-old who was a bit headstrong and needed plenty of schooling before he could go out on the trails.

When Jo had finished with his feet, Drifter barged to the stable door to look out and see what was going on.

"Manners!" Jo grumbled, pushing him back and managing to slide out safely.

Then it was the piebald, Comanche's turn to be mucked out and groomed – and so on, along the line of stables.

Soon the yard grew busy. There was the man with the trailer, delivering hay for the ponies, then a visit from the vet to do two inoculations, then the first of the trail riders, arriving early in brand new boots and jodhpurs.

Jo ran here and there, signing things, giving orders and generally being her bright and breezy self. Meanwhile, Krista worked on.

"Where's Jo?" Nathan Steele demanded when he arrived five minutes after his lesson was due to begin.

"Talking to the vet," Krista replied. "She's worried about Drifter's sore feet. I don't think he was shod properly at his last place."

Nathan sniffed. "I wanted to ride Drifter today. He's cool."

"Yeah, he's a good-looking pony," Krista agreed. "But he's not ready to be ridden yet."

"Says who?" Nathan retorted, ignoring Krista, going up to the new gelding's stable and opening the door.

"Hey!" Jo called from across the yard.

If Krista hadn't run up and closed the door quickly, Drifter would have barged past Nathan and bolted.

"Nathan, you're riding Shandy today as usual!" Jo told him firmly. "She's tacked up and ready."

"O-oh!" Nathan made a face. "Shandy's boring!"

Jo frowned. "Get a move on," she told him.

"Shandy's your level – a nice, quiet ride for someone who's still learning the basics!"

That told him! Krista thought, watching Jo lead Shandy out and hold her while Nathan mounted.

Nathan Steele was one of those I-know-best kids – a typical boy, Krista thought! She banished him from her head and got busy tacking up the ponies who were going out on the trail ride.

"That kid really winds me up!" Jo muttered after her lesson with Nathan. "He doesn't listen to a word I say! And now he wants to ride out on the trails, and I've had to tell his dad that Nathan is nowhere near ready to do that yet. He still has loads to learn.

They both drove off in a huff."

Krista held Jo's own horse, Apollo – a beautiful grey thoroughbred – while Jo mounted.

"Climb up on Misty and tag along," Jo invited, grinning at Krista as her face lit up. "You didn't think I'd get you to do all this work for nothing, did you?"

"Cool, thanks!" Krista grinned back. And she was up in the saddle of the strawberry roan in the blink of an eye, and then out on the trail, through the heather, down the lanes on to the beach and galloping on Misty along Whitton Sands.

Chapter Three

Who needs a magical pony? Krista asked herself.

That morning she'd flown along the beach on real life Misty. The waves had crashed against the shore, the pony's hooves had splashed through the shallows, sending up freezing white spray.

How lucky am I? she thought.

But still, as she cycled from the stables, back home along the cliff path, she slowed down as she reached the magic spot. Was it here by the rickety fence or here next to the gorse bush where she'd met Shining Star?

And had it really happened, or was it all in her daydreamy, restless mind?

Krista stopped pedalling and looked around. The sky was blue, with hardly any clouds, and definitely no silvery mist or shimmering light. *Huh.* Maybe she'd imagined

the flying pony. Maybe he didn't exist.

But then she did hear something – a rustling in the grass, or perhaps wings beating in the air. Krista held her breath and listened.

White gulls soared on the wind currents, high above. But her magical pony did not appear.

"Come back!" she whispered.

Be patient, Shining Star had told her.

Krista sighed, picked up her bike and pedalled on.

"There's a phone message for you," Krista's dad told her as soon as she got home.

She played the message.

"Hi, Krista. It's Jo. Can you ring me when you get in?"

"I already called her back," Krista's mum interrupted. "Apparently it's something to do with Drifter. Jo wants to know, did you bolt his door properly after you finished mucking him out this morning."

Krista's heart missed a beat. She picked up the phone and rang Jo.

"Hi, Krista. Thanks for ringing back. We've got a bit of a mystery here. Drifter's door is open and he's gone missing!"

"But I closed it, I'm sure I did!" Weird – her heart skipped a beat, then raced to catch up. *Try hard to remember.* "Yes, I kicked the bottom bolt into position, then I double-checked the top bolt. How can he have got out?"

"I don't know. Like I said, it's a mystery."

Jo sounded serious. "He was still here when we got back from the trail ride, but now his stable's empty."

"I'll come and help you look!" Krista told Jo. "We've got to find him!"

"No, listen. He can't have gone far, and he'll probably come back when he's hungry."

"What if he gets lost?" Hartfell moor was massive, there were steep hills and sheer drops over the cliff edge …

"Don't worry. It's my problem, Krista. I'll take a drive out on to the moor. I'm sure I'll find him."

"We'll start looking on this side of the moor," Krista insisted, glancing at her mum and dad, who both nodded. "If we see him, we'll ring you on your mobile."

And so it was agreed. Her parents set off from High Point Farm in different directions in their cars, while Krista took to the cliff path on her bike.

Where could Drifter be? Why would he wander off?

Of course, the little chestnut was new to the yard, and he was a high spirited pony liable to do something reckless like bolting when no one was looking. There again, horses didn't usually run away from shelter and food for no good reason.

Krista cycled hard up the path, eyes peeled for any sign of the runaway pony. *Shining Star, where are you when I need you?* she thought, looking up into the clear blue sky as she reached the magic spot. But there was no sign of help from the flying pony, not even the sound of wings beating.

Krista looked for Drifter everywhere she could think of – down hidden hollows on the moor where green grass grew and streams ran clear, in the shadow of rocky outcrops where the wind blew less fiercely, along lanes leading to other farms and cottages. Finally she cycled over to the stables, where she met up with Jo and her own mum and dad.

"I've spotted plenty of sheep on the hills, but no chestnut pony," Krista's mum reported.

"Me neither," her dad said.

By now it was late afternoon. Jo's face was creased with worry. "I don't understand it," she muttered. "It's like Drifter's vanished from the face of the earth!"

Krista went to check the pony's empty stable, as if wanting to make sure with her own eyes that he was gone.

In the stable next to Drifter's, Shandy

leaned over the door and whickered quietly.

"What happened, Shandy?" Krista whispered, knowing that the friendly little bay must have watched it all. "What did you see?"

Shandy nuzzled Krista's cheek with her soft muzzle, then suddenly clunked at the stable door with her hoof. *Look who's shown up!* she seemed to say.

Across the yard, a man in a shiny red Range Rover pulled up and came to talk to Jo.

"John Steele – Nathan's dad," he reminded her, shaking Jo by the hand.

Krista took in the short, stocky figure in the bright blue padded ski jacket – an older version of Nathan, with dark brown hair and the same know-it-all air. "What's he got to do with it?" she muttered to Shandy.

"Isn't my son back yet?" Mr Steele demanded, feet wide apart, hands on hips.

"Back from where?" Jo frowned.

Nathan's dad began stomping up and down the yard. "Back from his trail ride!"

"Uh-oh!" Krista began to work things out. *A missing boy ... a missing pony that wasn't ready to go out on the open trail.*

"What trail ride? What do you mean?" Jo demanded. "I haven't seen Nathan since the end of his lesson early this morning."

"Ah yes, well I drove him back here at lunchtime," John Steele admitted. "Nathan told me he had been allowed to join a trail ride on the little chestnut, and I thought it would do him good."

"Allowed to join a trail ride?" Jo echoed. "Mr Steele, do you really think I would let your son ride Drifter out on the open trail?"

"Why not?" the man said crossly. "Anyway, I thought it was all settled, and since there was no one about, I went to the tack room and found the chestnut's tack all properly labelled with his name. I know enough about horses to tack him up myself, no problem. I checked that Nathan was all set and ready to go before I left the yard."

Jo swallowed hard. "I should have checked the tack," she said to herself. "Why didn't I think of that?"

"None of us did," Krista's dad reminded her. "I guess we were all in such a panic about the missing pony."

"Now let's stay calm," Mr Steele interrupted. "There's probably no need to get worked up."

"Give me strength!" Jo muttered, turning her back on the visitor before she lashed out with words she might regret.

Krista's mum stepped in. "Let's get this straight. You thought Nathan was going out on a guided ride – at what time?"

"Round about one-thirty," Mr Steele said, folding his arms then looking uncomfortably down at the ground.

"At one-thirty, on Drifter," Krista's mum repeated unsteadily.

"... Who's only been here for less than a week," Krista cut in. "Who's only three and not properly schooled. And Nathan's a beginner!"

"It's almost five o'clock," Krista's mum said, checking her watch. "And you've only just shown up to see if they're back?"

"Nathan said he'd call me. I thought he must be having a great time," Mr Steele shrugged.

"Give me strength!" Jo muttered again.

"Nathan must have snuck out of the yard without anyone noticing," Krista's dad told him. "People have been out looking for the pony all afternoon. No one's seen any sign of him, or of your son either."

Mr Steele glanced from one worried face to the next. "Ri-ight!" he said, sucking through his teeth. "So there was no guided ride. Nathan made it all up. But they can't have gone far, surely!"

"Not far!" Jo burst out at last. "Have you any idea how big and dangerous these moors are at night, Mr Steele? Don't you realise that there are hundred-metre cliffs to fall down, and tides that can come in and cut you off if you're daft enough to ride out without a guide?"

"You're laying it on thick to panic me and make me feel bad," Steele protested. "Nathan's a good kid. He won't do anything stupid."

The three adults shook their heads.

"You just can't get through to him," Krista's mum sighed.

But Krista wouldn't leave it like that. She walked straight up to Mr Steele and looked him in the eye. "Drifter could stumble out there on the moor and break a leg," she insisted. "It's going to be dark soon, and it'll get cold. Nathan should never have ridden him out alone. And now they're lost. And the worst that could happen is that they might both die!"

Chapter Four

Late that afternoon Krista's dad rounded up six more people to go out on to Hartfell and search for Drifter and Nathan.

The searchers were sheep farmers and owners of holiday cottages on the rocky coast.

"Let's not involve the police until we have to," Mr Steele had insisted, still refusing to believe Krista's harsh warning. "I need to talk to my wife first. Besides, these farmers know the country better than anyone. I'm sure they'll find my son safe and sound."

The willing neighbours had gone out on foot to cover every metre of ground before nightfall.

"I don't care about Nathan," Krista told Spike, sitting cross legged on the grass at the bottom of their garden, where she'd gone soon after her mum had brought her home. "It's Drifter I'm worried about."

The tame hedgehog paddled in the dish of drinking water she'd taken out for him.

Krista sighed. "I know – I should be worried about Nathan too, shouldn't I?"

Spike splished and splashed happily.

"If I was a nice person, I'd feel sorry for him, out there all alone." Only, it was hard, knowing that this was all Nathan's own fault. "Look, it's already getting dark!" she pointed out.

This suited Spike, who liked the night time and could find his way through all the hedgerows and ditches by moonlight, but it was bad news for Nathan and Drifter. "Now Mr Steele will *have* to call the police!"

Krista's dad was still out on the moor searching for the missing pony and his rider, along with Jo and John Steele, plus all the neighbours.

"What if ..." Krista gasped, struck by a sudden thought.

She jumped up from the grass and looked out beyond the garden, up the hill to where the path ran along the cliff edge. In spite of the fading light, she could still make out her magic spot.

"Yes, that's it!" she cried. Things had grown really serious since she'd last cycled over the brow of the hill early that afternoon. Surely now would be the time to run up there and wait for Shining Star to appear!

It was dusk. A mist was creeping in off the sea.

"Don't even think about it!" Krista's mum had just come out into the garden to find Krista. She'd read the excited gleam in her daughter's eye. "Whatever you're planning, you have to leave it until tomorrow!"

"But Mum!" Krista protested. She itched

to run through the garden gate, out on to the open moor.

"It's almost dark!" her mum insisted. "You're not going anywhere until you've had a good night's sleep."

"I can't sleep, I'm too upset! … Mum, just let me … I have to …!"

"You have to what?" There was a no-nonsense tone in Krista's mum's voice that Krista knew not to argue with.

"I have to – oh, never mind!" *She'll never believe me,* Krista thought. *"I have to go to the spot and meet my magical pony!"* What grown-up would believe that?

"Come inside," her mum said softly, taking her by the hand.

"I'm scared, Mum," Krista said, trailing up the lawn, glancing over her shoulder at the cliff path.

At the kitchen door, her mum gave her a quick hug. "Me too," she confessed.

*

Mist covered the moor. Jo had called off the search until morning.

Krista lay in bed, listening to the waves roll in at high tide. Low voices in the kitchen told her that her dad had come home and there was still no news of the missing boy and pony.

"Wait until daylight … police have been informed …coastguard … who knows!"

Krista's stomach twisted itself in knots. She crept to the window and tried her hardest to make Shining Star appear in his cloud of shimmering, silver dust.

"Imagine if it was Krista out there at this time of night. We'd be out of our minds with worry!" her mum murmured to her dad as they came upstairs to bed. The bedroom door closed and the house fell silent.

"Shining Star, you have to come!" Krista pleaded, opening her window so that the flying pony might hear. "You told me to be patient, but how can I when I know that Drifter's lost and alone?"

There was no answer, except for the crash of the waves.

"Is it because I'm not on the magic spot?" she asked. "Is that why you won't come?"

The wind blew the window shut and Krista saw the reflection of her own face – pale, with big, staring eyes.

"I have to go!" she decided. Out into

the dark night, into the swirling fog.

Quickly she pulled on her trousers and a warm fleece, shoved her feet into her riding boots, then climbed through the window on to the long sloping roof of the kitchen. Praying that she didn't slip and fall, she crept on all fours to the edge, then dropped to the ground.

Easy! she breathed. But was she brave enough to plunge into the darkness, without stars or moon to guide her?

Then she thought of beautiful Drifter stranded far from home, surrounded by sounds that scared him – the hoot of an owl, the bark of foxes, the echo of waves crashing into a dark cave.

She found herself running up the path, not able to see the edge of the cliff, but knowing it was there. She heard the crunch of gravel under her feet, smelt the salt in the air.

Then Krista stopped. Now she was a tiny figure, standing on the brow of the dark hill, gazing up into the black sky.

Was it really there – that faint silver shimmer, the fall of glittering dust on to her face? And were those wings beating through the air, or only the wind?

Krista squeezed her eyes tight shut then opened them again.

Shining Star came out of the mist, trailing his silvery blue light, more beautiful than ever.

His neck arched proudly, his outspread wings beat gently as he hovered overhead.

"Good," he said to Krista. "You came when you were needed."

"Oh, Shining Star!" she gasped, reaching her arms out towards him. "Thank heavens you're here. Such a bad thing has happened!"

Chapter Five

"Drifter is a young pony. He doesn't know his way around." The words spilled from Krista's mouth in a rush. "Nathan should never have taken him out of the yard. We've looked everywhere, and now it's the middle of the night and they're still out there somewhere!"

Shining Star listened quietly. "They're in great danger," he told her.

Krista gasped. "You know where they are?"

"No. But there is trouble ahead." The magical pony had alighted on the path and folded his wings against his sides. "I feel it crackling in the air – danger and fear!"

She shivered. "What can we do? I'd hate it if anything bad happened to Drifter!"

"And the boy, Nathan?"

"Yes, him too."

"Then we will go and search," the pony said, spreading his wings once more.

"Are we going to fly through the dark?" Krista asked. The thought made her dizzy.

Shining Star tossed his head. "Are you afraid?"

She nodded.

"Don't be. I will take good care of you. Remember, I chose you."

Gathering courage, Krista took hold of the pony's mane and eased herself on to his back.

"Why?" she wanted to know. "Why did you choose me?"

"I did not choose," he said, then turned his head sideways to look at her. "My world is called Galishe. There is a council of wise creatures there who decides such things."

"And can these creatures all do magic and talk and fly like you?"

"Too many questions," Shining Star replied, looking up into the dark sky. "But you must understand that when most others from your world meet me, they see only an ordinary pony, without wings. To them I am not special. Only you know who I truly am."

Krista nodded and held tight. Then Shining Star beat his wings. They rose from the cliff

My Magical Pony

into the murky fog, out across Whitton Bay.

The damp mist clung to Krista's face and hair, and as she glanced around she could see only thick cloud. But the pony's wings sheltered her and soothed her with their steady beats as she felt him rise higher and higher until at last they broke through the top of the clouds into the starlit heavens.

Then the air grew clear and soft, like dark blue velvet, and the pony trailed his sparkling dust in a wide arc through the sky, while Krista looked in wonder at the stars.

Some were bright silver, some gold, some surrounded by a red or green haze, some twinkling, still others blazing with a fierce light.

And then, much closer, there was the moon! It was a full disc sailing through the sky. Krista held her breath as Shining Star hovered for a few moments to let her take in its beauty.

"Oh!" she sighed. Below her was cloud. Above, the moon and stars.

Then Shining Star turned and plunged earthwards, back through the cold clouds.

"See over there – the sun is rising!" Krista cried as her magical pony circled Whitton Bay.

There was a glow of pink light, creeping slowly on to the horizon to the east.

"The tide is out," Shining Star observed.

"Are we going to land on the beach?" Krista asked, her voice high, her whole body tingling with excitement.

The pony waited to catch an air current that would float them gently towards the sands. "It won't be light for a while, but we will search the shore as best we can."

"Whooo!" Krista's stomach did a flip like it did when she rode a roller-coaster. The earth seemed to rush up to meet them.

But Shining Star landed safely, spreading his cloud of silvery glitter across the pale white sand. He waited for his rider to slide off his back, then quietly folded his wings.

For a while Krista stood by the pony's side, wondering what she should do.

"Even if Nathan and Drifter came this way yesterday afternoon, the tide will already have washed their footprints away," she pointed out.

"We should look among the rocks," Shining Star decided, picking his way carefully over the pebbles that bordered the beach.

Krista stumbled after him. It wasn't easy to

see where to put her feet. "I think the farmers came down here to look before it got dark," she explained. "And some people from the holiday cottages as well. They didn't find anything."

Shining Star turned to wait. "What next?"

Krista shook her head. "I don't know. Maybe Nathan rode Drifter further than this. Or maybe Drifter spooked and bolted."

"Let's fly again. That way we can cover more ground."

Nodding eagerly, Krista climbed up and clung tight.

This time, Shining Star scarcely rose above the height of the rocks and coves lining the bay. He skimmed the earth while Krista peered down into the shadowy places.

"Stop here!" she would say, and the pony would land. She would slide to the ground then run into a narrow crevice between two tall rocks, take a look and emerge with a shake of her head. "Nothing."

Then they would fly again, checking each hidden place until they reached the western end of the bay.

"What lies beyond here?" Shining Star asked.

By now the sun was clear of the horizon, rising higher and burning off the thin morning mist.

"Hardly anything," Krista replied. "There are no more houses or roads, not even a cliff path. It's just a long stretch of rocky land and then the sea."

She turned to Shining Star and saw that he was alert, ears pricked forward, neck arched.

"Nathan wouldn't take Drifter on to Black Point," she whispered, suddenly gripped by a new fear. "He'd have to be crazy!"

"Let's check," Shining Star decided, waiting for Krista to mount. "The danger in the air has grown stronger," he warned her. "You must be prepared."

In the new, pale light, Shining Star and Krista flew out to sea, cleared the furthest point of Whitton Bay and carried on along the finger of bare rock that travelled half a kilometre out to sea then ended in a terrifying sheer drop into fierce waves.

"Nobody comes to Black Point," Krista murmured. "It's too dangerous."

"Somebody is here!" Shining Star insisted. His wings beat harder as he battled a strong wind coming in off the sea. "I can't see where, so we must land and search again."

Unsteadily the pony flew to the brow of a steep rocky hill and found a place to land. Krista dismounted. She saw the sea moving in on them from three sides, rushing to meet the black rocks. She felt the wind almost blow her off her feet.

"We must take care," Shining Star warned her, as he turned his back to the weak sun and headed west.

Chapter Six

Black Point spooked Krista. It was a wild place where nothing grew and no one came. There were bad stories, of ships being wrecked and sailors drowning.

"I hear many voices asking for help," Shining Star told her. He stopped to listen. "No," he said. "They cry out from another time, long ago."

"The dead sailors!" Krista shivered. She too imagined the desperate shouts, the splitting of ships' timbers on the rocks, the suck of the waves as they dragged men down.

What am I doing here? she asked herself. *What if Mum goes into my room and finds that I'm not there?*

A strong wave crashed against a rock to their left, sending white spray high into the air.

"Wait," Shining Star ordered. He turned to look behind them.

When Krista turned too, she made out a lonely figure on horseback, preparing to follow them along Black Point. "It's Jo on Apollo!" she told Shining Star. "She must have had the same idea as us!"

There was nothing for it but to wait, watching the sun rise behind Jo, beginning to feel its warmth.

"Krista, what are you doing out here?"

Jo demanded as she reined Apollo to a halt. She looked down on the girl and a dappled grey pony. "Who's this stranger?"

"This is Star!" Krista replied quickly. "I found him wandering on the moor." Would Jo notice anything strange about her magic horse, or would it be as Shining Star had said, that his wings were invisible to everyone except Krista?

Jo looked at him and nodded. "Hmm, he's a pretty little thing. He must have broken out of his field somewhere. I don't recognise him though."

"No, he just kind of adopted me," Krista told her with a short sigh of relief. Then she changed the subject. "I came out early to look for Drifter. I couldn't sleep."

"Me neither. Not a wink. I waited until I heard that the mountain rescue people and the coastguards had been alerted late last night, then I saddled Apollo and came out."

"Do you think Nathan would bring Drifter way out here?" Krista asked, looking to right and left at the sea surrounding them.

"It's one place we didn't search yesterday."

Jo dismounted and Krista could tell from her tired, drawn face how serious the situation was. "It's not looking good," she confessed. "I would have expected Drifter to bring Nathan back before nightfall if he'd been able to. A pony can always find his way home."

"So you think Drifter's been hurt?"

As they talked, big Apollo bent his head to inspect Shining Star. He sniffed at the pony's face and neck, then jerked his head back as if he'd encountered something powerful and strange. He skittered sideways.

Uh-oh! Krista thought. *Apollo knows!*

"Stand still, 'Pollo!" Jo ordered, as her phone began to ring and she reached into her pocket to pull it out and answer it.

A deep frown formed on her face. "It's your dad!" she mouthed at Krista.

"Uh-oh!" This time Krista said it out loud.

Shining Star waited quietly at her side.

"Yes … Yes, she's here … OK, I'll bring her straight back!" Jo said into the phone. She sighed as she put the phone back into her pocket. "You left without telling them!"

Slowly Krista nodded. "They were still asleep."

"Have you any idea how worried they are?"

"I know. I'm sorry."

"Your mum was frantic."

"I said I'm sorry." Miserably, Krista hung her head. Everything had gone wrong. She'd been stupid not to leave a note at least.

"I promised I'd take you back to my place because it's nearer." Jo sounded as if she wasn't prepared to argue. She frowned at Krista then at the pony. "Do you think you can ride him bareback?"

If only you knew! Krista thought. *Not only bareback, but through the air, high into the sky, to look at the moon!* "I'll give it a go," she said meekly.

As Krista went up to Shining Star and took

hold of his mane, she murmured in his ear. "I'm sorry we didn't find Drifter."

The pony lowered his head. "I understand. You must go back," he told her.

She looked closely and thought she saw a glimmer of disappointment in his eye that made her want to change her mind and carry on with the search.

"Get a move on, Krista!" Jo urged. "The sooner I get you back safe and sound, the sooner I can get out here and start looking again!"

Yes, everything had gone wrong! Krista's legs felt stiff and unwilling as she swung herself on to Shining Star's back. She plodded after Jo and Apollo with a heavy heart.

Chapter Seven

"We were so worried!" Krista's mum cried once Krista had got back. "What on earth were you thinking?"

Nothing that I could explain to you or make you believe! Krista said to herself.

She'd ridden Shining Star along Black Point to Whitton Bay, and back up to Hartfell, following in Apollo's footsteps until they reached the gate to the stable yard. Here, Krista had dismounted and given the pony's neck a quick stroke. "Sorry!" she said again.

He'd leaned his head towards her and told her he understood. He had gazed at her long and hard, then turned and trotted away.

"Shouldn't someone catch that pony?" Krista's dad had wondered as he ran to the gate carrying a lead-rope.

Jo had said there would be time for that later. First they had to find Nathan and Drifter.

And now Krista was smothered by her mum's kisses, suffocated by her hugs.

"We guessed this was where you'd be!" she cried. "But honestly, love, when we went into your room and found your bed empty, it was such a shock!"

"Mum, I kept thinking about Drifter being

lost – I couldn't get him out of my head!"

"And so you went and risked your neck to go and find him!" her dad said, shaking his head in disbelief. "In the dead of night, apparently. It's a good job Jo came across you when she did, and stopped you doing anything even crazier!"

"Whose was that grey pony?" her mum demanded, stepping back to let Krista breathe at last.

"Nobody's – I don't know!" Krista answered honestly. "I don't think he lives round here."

Luckily for her, there were too many things going on for people to worry about the mystery of Shining Star.

As Krista's dad told her firmly that from now on she had to stay on the yard while the search went on, Jo dealt with phone calls from the mountain rescue and coastguard teams. Then a police Land Rover arrived with Mr and Mrs Steele.

John Steele strode straight across to Jo. "Is there any news?" he begged.

"Nothing yet."

"No information from the coastguards?"

Jo shook her head. "They've been out since dawn, but they haven't seen anything. The mountain rescue people are bringing a helicopter over. It should be here in an hour."

"This is all my fault!" Mr Steele muttered.

Surprised, Krista stared at Nathan's dad. This was a change from yesterday!

"I should've stopped to think, I know that now. But Nathan was so keen on riding the chestnut pony, and he's had a tough time lately, what with us moving house and him having a new school. I just thought that cutting him a bit of slack might give him a boost."

"Wrong!" Jo shook her head. "We have rules on this yard for very good reasons!"

"I know that now." John Steele rubbed his forehead then ran his hand across his eyes.

"Listen, Jo, my wife is in bits. Isn't there a single piece of good news I might be able to pass on to her?"

"Not yet. But we're doing everything we possibly can."

"Let's go," Krista's dad said quietly to her mum. Everyone could see how upset the Steeles were. Mrs Steele sat huddled in the police car, while her desperate husband went from one person to the next.

"You stay here, Krista," her mum ordered. "Your dad and I are going to drive out and join the search."

Doing everything they possibly can! Krista thought. She took up a fork and began to muck out the nearest stable. *Everything, except following the magical pony to the place where Drifter and Nathan are hidden!*

By ten o'clock the tension on the stable yard was so bad that Krista felt stifled. She almost had to remind herself to breathe.

Everyone, except Mr and Mrs Steele and the police officer who had driven the Land Rover, was out on the moors. Nathan's dad had stayed with his mum, who had begged him not to leave her. A rescue helicopter flew overhead, the clatter of its blades disturbing the ponies in their paddocks.

Leaning on her fork, Krista yawned. Being up all night had exhausted her and made her feel light-headed. But still she'd mucked out all the stables and laid fresh straw. Now all there was to do was wait.

As she stood, she heard the police woman speak into her radio then turn to Mr Steele. "What colour is the missing pony?" she asked.

"Drifter's a chestnut."

"Not grey?" the officer checked.

"No, definitely a rich, deep brown. Why?"

"The helicopter just spotted a grey pony out at the western end of Whitton Bay, but it's obviously a false alarm." Speaking again into the radio, she told the pilot to ignore the sighting.

Krista took a deep breath. *That must be Shining Star!* she thought. *He's heading back to Black Point alone!*

"I can't stand much more of this!" Mrs Steele wailed, getting out of the car and running blindly towards the gate, then leaning on it and bursting into loud sobs.

Krista went quietly towards the police officer in the car. "Tell the helicopter to search Black Point," she insisted.

"Why? What do you know about it?" John Steele broke in.

"Nothing. I'm just guessing. But it's one place they haven't looked properly yet." No way could Krista tell them that a magical flying pony had led her there and felt the danger crackling in the air.

The woman in uniform frowned. She'd obviously heard about Krista's pre-dawn adventure. "You've caused enough trouble for one day," she told her firmly.

For a few moments Krista closed her eyes in defeat. She'd been grounded. She'd promised her mum and dad that she wouldn't be going anywhere until they came back. What could she do except keep busy and wait for news?

So she went into the tack room where rows of bridles hung from hooks, and began to sweep the floor, until a woman's voice interrupted her.

"You're Krista – Nathan's friend – aren't you?"

Krista looked up and recognised Mrs Steele. "Kind of," she mumbled. Not that she would have called Nathan Steele a friend exactly, even before he'd done this reckless ride on Drifter, and definitely not since.

"He's always talking about you, Krista,"

Mrs Steele insisted in a choked voice, her eyes red and swollen from crying. She was a tall woman, with straight, fair hair, muffled up in a waxed jacket and checked scarf. "He says you're the best rider on the yard."

Krista looked up in surprise. "Nathan did?"

"Yes, he really admired – *admires* you!"

"I never knew that!" Krista stopped sweeping to consider what Nathan's mum had said.

"He's a shy boy, so he probably wouldn't come out with it to your face."

Shy? This too was news.

"Sometimes he finds it hard to fit in. That's why he just marches in and does his own thing. Anyway, I was glad when he came home a couple of weeks ago and told me you were his friend. And thank you for what you tried to do earlier this morning."

Krista sighed and nodded. "I'm sure they'll find him soon."

This made Mrs Steele lower her head and swallow back a sob. When she finally spoke, the words came out as a desperate prayer – "I hope you're right, Krista. I really do!"

Chapter Eight

Krista swept the tack room floor then polished the bridles until they shone. The clock on the wall ticked loudly, and every minute seemed to drag.

Poor Drifter! she thought. Then, a bit later – *Poor Nathan!*

She stopped working and looked up. *Poor Nathan. Did I just say that?*

It was the first time Krista had spared a thought for the missing boy rather than Drifter, and it was because of what his mum had told her.

I guess he was lonely, she realised, *and I never really made an effort to be his friend.*

She thought of Shining Star making his way alone to Black Point, certain that this was the place where they would find Drifter and Nathan. Then she looked around at the neat rows of tack. *This is no good! I should be out there with my magical pony!* she told herself.

"What did you say?" Mr Steele had wandered in without Krista noticing. He was striding up and down, unable to keep still.

"Nothing. I didn't mean to talk out loud." Excusing herself, Krista fled the room. Out in the yard, she saw the helicopter slowly circling the moorland over Hartfell, far away from where it should be looking.

"That's it!" she said. And this time she didn't care if anyone overheard. She didn't care any more about the trouble she'd caused, or what her mum had told her about staying where she was – she couldn't just wait here and do nothing!

There was an old bike propped up against some bales of straw in the barn, and Krista went to fetch it. She was astride the saddle and pedalling out of the gate before anyone saw her. In any case, the police officer was using the radio and Mr Steele was busy comforting his wife.

"I'm coming!" Krista yelled into the wind, knowing that Shining Star couldn't possibly hear her, and yet needing to tell him that she was on her way. Nothing would stop her now.

The old bike clanked and clattered along the lane on to the road. From here, Krista could look down at the sweeping coastline and up on to the great hump of purple moorland rising to a rocky horizon.

She had to make a decision – should she head for the magic spot and hope that Shining Star would retrace his steps and come to find her? Or should she race ahead to join him on Black Point?

Black Point! She decided there was no time to lose, and the quickest way was down to the cliff-top car park, where she would leave the bike and scramble down to Whitton Sands on foot. From there, she would run along the beach and clamber on to the bleak finger of rock pointing out to sea.

So Krista set off down the hill on a mad, screeching journey, taking the bends without brakes, leaning into the curves, sensing that every lost second was vital. A small team of local searchers saw her speed by, stopped for a moment, then carried on trekking across the heather, beating at the bushes, trying to uncover even the smallest clue.

Soon she came to the big square of tarmac overlooking the bay. Propping the bike against a car park sign, Krista set off down the wooden steps to the beach some thirty metres below. She jumped the last three steps on to the soft sand.

Breathless now, she paused to look around. Here, high on the beach, the sand was dry and littered with dark bands of dried seaweed and pieces of driftwood. Lower down, the sea was licking at the shore, gradually breaking higher with every incoming wave.

"Tide's coming in," Krista muttered. She began to run along the beach, choosing the firm sand closest to the water's edge. At the western edge of the bay, she climbed back on to the rocks, treading through rock-pools to reach the long outcrop where she knew she would find Shining Star.

At first she could see no sign of the magical pony – only the desolate rocks and the sea whipping up waves at the furthest point. She felt the wind strengthen, and remembered the ghostly voices of the drowned sailors. For a second her courage faltered.

Then she saw her pony.

Shining Star was standing at the far end

of Black Point, his white wings outstretched. He turned towards her, surrounded by his magic mist, silver shimmering on to the black rock where he stood.

Krista ran to meet him. "I came back!" she shouted above the wind.

Shining Star raised his beautiful head and tossed his mane. "I knew you would," he said gently. "When the time was right, and your heart was true."

Together again, Krista and Shining Star searched the narrow coves of Black Point.

"There are too many voices," the pony told her. "The voices of drowned men, coming off the sea then lost in the caves under the ground."

"You mean voices of ghosts?" Krista felt the same dread as before creep into her bones. How come the drowned sailors could still speak to the pony? "I can't hear them!"

"You can if you listen!" Shining Star said, bracing himself against the wind and sheltering Krista with his wings.

The wind gusted and its sound surrounded her. It wailed and turned into human sounds.

"We are washed against the rocks! The ship breaks up .... May the Lord deliver us!"

"Oh!" Krista gasped.

"Help me, I cannot swim! ... The waters close above me!"

Krista blocked out the wailing voices with her hands. "Those poor men!" she cried.

"Hundreds of souls," Shining Star told her. "They block the voices of those who are still alive and in danger."

"Are we sure that Nathan and Drifter are really here?" Krista asked. She longed to climb on to the pony's back and fly away from this place.

"*Save us!*" the voices cried.

"They are here," Shining Star insisted. "We must go down to the shore and check the underground caves before the tide comes in."

Krista clenched her hands into fists as if to fight her fears. "Let's do it!" she whispered.

The rocks were wet and slimy; their sharp points grazed her knees when she slipped and fell. A short way out to sea, creeping closer with each minute, the white waves crashed against the land.

Krista hurried from one tiny cove to the

next. She peered under dark overhangs, crawling deep under the rocks into dry caves, and coming out to tell Shining Star the bad news. "No," she would report. "They're not there."

After ten minutes or so, with the ghosts still chattering in her ear, doubt again crept into Krista's head. *What if we're looking in the wrong place after all? Maybe this isn't any good and we should get out of here while we can.*

So she turned and pleaded with the pony to try something new. "Why don't you call for Drifter? I know it's a long shot, but perhaps he'll hear."

Shining Star nodded. "You must listen hard for a reply."

Lifting his head and stretching out his neck, the pony bared his teeth in a loud, shrill whinny.

The wind took the noise and whipped it into the air, the waves drowned it.

Krista listened, but there was no answering call. "Try again!" she urged.

Once more, Shining Star made the call.

Krista strained her ears. There was a lull in the wind, and for a split second, the waves stopped crashing against the rocks.

And there it was – a faint, high sound – the unmistakable whinny of another horse, answering Shining Star!

Chapter Nine

"You were right!" Krista gasped. "That was Drifter answering you!"

The flying pony nodded and led the way, following the direction of Drifter's reply.

"At least he's alive!" Krista murmured, trying to block out the ghostly voices and concentrate on the missing pony. "But what's wrong with Nathan? Why isn't he coming to meet us?"

"We'll soon know," Shining Star promised. He went with his ears pricked, his dark brown eyes alert.

Krista followed, but she grew more afraid of the waves with every step. "The tide's coming in fast!" she cried, as the water swirled up around her ankles and frothed over the rocks.

Out to sea she spotted a small boat. It bobbed through the choppy waves, cruising along the coastline at a steady rate. "There's the coastguard!" she told Shining Star. She waved and yelled at the top of her voice, but the boat sailed on.

There was nothing for it but to go on alone.

Soon the pony stopped at the entrance to a long, narrow cove that cut into the rock. He gave one final whinny, and then Drifter appeared from a dark cave at the back of the cove.

He was a dreadful sight. His smooth mane was tangled, there was sand in his glossy chestnut coat, and a bad gash down the side of his neck.

"Poor boy!" Krista breathed, forgetting the crashing waves and the wailing voices of the dead sailors. She ran into the cove to meet him.

Close to, she could see that his coat was stiff with dried salt-water and he was shaking from head to foot. He reared as she came near, refusing to let her take hold of his reins.

"Go and find the boy," Shining Star told her. He approached Drifter and began to speak with him and calm him.

Krista went on, splashing through a shallow pool at the entrance to the cave, then ducking her head and creeping forward. It was dark under here, and the roof grew lower. When she raised her voice to call Nathan's name, an echo came back.

"Nathan!" Krista yelled.

Nay-than-than-than!

Then, *"The ship is lost, and all souls on board! Save us!"*

Krista gritted her teeth and forced herself

to carry on. In the dark she slid knee-deep into another pool, then scrambled out, up on to a ledge of rock. Suddenly she had a strange, prickly feeling that she wasn't alone, that someone was nearby. "Nathan, is that you?" she asked, with a tight band of fear around her chest.

"Save us-us-us!"

... *Is that you-oo-oo?*

"Who's there?" a trembling voice asked.

... *There-ere-ere!*

"Nathan, it's me – Krista!" It was too dark to see. She felt the rough rock with her fingertips, easing herself along the dry ledge. "Are you OK?" she cried.

"Krista, help me!"

"Aah!" Her hand touched something soft, and she pulled it back quickly.

Then Nathan reached out and grabbed her arm. "I can't move!" he cried. "My leg won't work. Krista, you've got to get me out of here!"

Krista ran from the cave to give Shining Star the news. She found him standing beside Drifter. Behind them, the waves stormed against the rocks.

"Nathan's in the cave. He's hurt his leg. How are we going to get him out?"

"Drifter has told me what happened," the flying pony explained. "He says the boy's leg is broken."

"He's very scared," Krista said. She'd never seen anyone so frightened in her whole life.

"Get me out of here!" Nathan had pleaded.

Krista had just been able to make out his face in the darkness, and she'd let him hang on to her arm until he'd begun to calm down.

"I spent the whole night here," he whimpered. "It's so cold. And I'm hearing voices. They won't go away!"

"Don't worry about them," Krista insisted, sounding braver than she felt. "Everyone hears them. They won't do you any harm."

"Drifter stayed here with me." Nathan was in tears as he told her the full story. "He didn't need to stay, but he kind of stood guard at the entrance to the cave when the tide came in. I thought we were both going to drown!"

"But you didn't!" Krista soothed him. "How come you ended up here in the first place?"

"It was all my fault. I was up on the cliff path and I wanted Drifter to canter. I forced him. Then something in a ditch spooked him

– a bird, or a rabbit – I don't know. Anyway, Drifter took off. He galloped too fast and we kind of slipped over the edge of the cliff together …"

"Is that when Drifter cut his neck?" Krista interrupted.

Nathan nodded. "We slid all the way down to the beach, and by this time he was so scared he took off again, right along here. I couldn't stop him. I just hung on. Then he raced up on to the rocks and slipped again. This time he threw me off and I landed wrong and that's when I hurt my leg. I just about managed to drag myself in here to find shelter …"

"It's OK, don't say any more." Krista tried to stop Nathan from breaking into tears.

"You have to stay here, OK! I'm going to get help."

"Don't go!" he pleaded. "The tide's coming in again. I can hear it."

"Just stay. I promise I'll come back!"

Nathan had sighed, then nodded, and Krista had crept back towards the daylight, out into the fresh air.

"The cave is too low for me to enter," Shining Star decided. His voice was calm. He didn't let the roar of the waves hurry him.

Krista felt the wind tear at her clothes and whip her hair from her face. Spray from the sea filled the air.

"Drifter, you were amazing!" Krista whispered,

tears coming to her eyes as she gently wiped the sand from the wound on his neck.

The young pony lowered his head quietly.

"We only have a short time before the waves drive us back," Shining Star went on. "So, Krista, you must find a way to help the boy out on to the beach. Can he walk?"

She shook her head. "Maybe if I can find something for him to use as a crutch," she said. "And he can lean on me as well ..."

Shining Star nodded. "Perhaps driftwood would do?"

"I'll see what I can find!"

Forcing herself back into the cave and remembering her promise to Nathan, Krista ran back into the shadows. Water dripped from the roof of the cave and the voices called again, as she began to rummage amongst a heap of tangled seaweed caught in a crevice in the rocks.

"Krista?" Nathan called from deep within the cave.

"Yes, it's me. I'm looking for a long stick to help us!"

"Hurry!" he pleaded.

"Try to ease yourself down from the ledge." Krista tugged at the pile of rubbish, took hold of a smooth piece of wood and pulled hard.

"I don't know if I can … OK, I'm doing it … ouch!"

The plank was long enough for the task. Krista grasped it, stooped and crept back into the cave.

She found Nathan at ground level, slumped against a rock and holding on to his left leg. "Grab this and put it under your arm," she ordered. "Now sling the other one round my shoulder. Come on, Nathan, you've got to try!"

Waves thundered on to the rocks, the exit from the cave was misted over with white spray.

"We can do it!" Krista cried, stumbling as she bore Nathan's weight.

Nathan limped heavily, crying out with pain.

"Drifter and Shining Star are waiting for us on the rocks!"

"I don't think I can! Krista, I'm not going to make it!"

"You are!" she told him. A strong wave hit the shore and swirled up into the cave. It smacked into them, tugging at their legs, foaming around their knees. Krista gasped. Then she pulled herself together. "Come on, Nathan! We've got this far – we're not going to give in now!"

Chapter Ten

There was water everywhere.

It sucked in and out of the rock pools and dragged the pebbles from the shore. And then fresh waves came crashing in, again and again, swallowing up the ground from under Krista and Nathan's feet.

But there was blue sky above their heads now – they were clear of the cave.

"Good!" Krista gasped. Water swirled against her, up to her waist. "Look! Drifter and Shining Star are waiting!"

The ponies stood on a windswept rock,

gazing anxiously into the mouth of the cave. When Shining Star saw two figures stagger clear, he plunged into the water to meet them.

"Tell the boy to climb on to my back!" he ordered, standing firm as the waves swept against him.

"You have to mount!" she repeated, dragging Nathan into position and hoisting him up.

Pride made the boy grit his teeth and not cry out. "Is it safe?" he asked.

Krista nodded. She felt a strong wave almost knock her off balance. "Hang on to his mane. Believe me. He will take you out of here!"

"And you must climb on too," Shining Star instructed. "I will carry you both. Be quick!"

But Krista shook her head. "What about Drifter?"

"He will take his chance along the rocks."

"No, he can't do that alone. I'll go with him!"

"It's dangerous," Shining Star warned.

"I won't leave him!" she cried.

The waves drowned their voices. Krista's magical pony tossed his mane and looked deep into her eyes. "I will take the boy," he agreed. "And you will ride Drifter."

So Krista scrambled up on to the nearest rock in time to escape the next high wave. She glanced back at Shining Star bearing

Nathan, spreading his wings and flying clear of the water, hovering in his bright mist, his head turned towards her.

"I'm OK!" she yelled. She scrambled towards the chestnut pony, whose eyes rolled with fear. "Easy," she told him, hooking her foot into the stirrup.

Drifter held steady as she swung into the saddle.

Krista turned him towards the east. If only Drifter had wings, like Shining Star – wings that would lift them into the calm clear sky, out of danger.

But, as the magical pony beat his wings and flew ahead with the injured boy, Krista had to help Drifter pick his way across the treacherous rocks, slowly, one faltering step at a time.

Drifter slid and slipped. He shook his poor head and shied away from the sea spray. Krista held the reins steady, though they plunged deep into pools. Drifter reared and skittered sideways. "Easy, boy!" she murmured.

Ahead of them, Shining Star beat his wings gently, soaring over the rocks into Whitton Bay.

"We have to reach the bay before the tide comes right up!" Krista knew that the waves would soon swallow the last of the dry land and leave them stranded on Black Point.

But Drifter was going as fast as he could, battling the water as it swirled around his hooves.

"You're a good, brave boy!" she breathed.

Slowly but surely the curve of the bay came into sight.

"Yes!" she whispered. "Keep going, Drifter!"

The wind and waves battered them, forced them to battle on, then "Yes!" Krista said again.

Drifter reached the summit of the rock

overlooking the dry sands of Whitton Bay. He stumbled, then regained his balance.

"We did it!" Krista murmured. She slid to the ground and led the brave chestnut pony down on to the beach.

"What happened?" a dazed Nathan asked.

He had no memory of flying through the air on Shining Star. All he knew was, he was safe on Whitton Sands with Drifter and

Krista, riding bareback on a strange grey pony whom he'd never seen before.

The magical pony seemed to smile.

And then there were rescue teams running down the steps on to the beach, and an ambulance driving towards them – people everywhere, yelling at Krista and Nathan – shouts of relief rising above the roar of the waves.

"Don't move!" Krista told Nathan.

There were paramedics with a stretcher, gently lifting Nathan from the grey pony, telling Krista she'd done a great job and probably saved the boy's life.

"Thank you!" Nathan whispered.

"That's OK. I'll come and see you later, in hospital."

He nodded and closed his eyes.

Then Jo and the Steeles showed up in the police Land Rover. "The coastguard spotted activity on Black Point and radioed for assistance," the police officer explained.

Mr and Mrs Steele thanked Krista over and over then climbed into the ambulance with their son.

Jo jumped out of the Land Rover and ran to Drifter.

"He's cut his neck!" Krista explained. "But he stayed with Nathan all night. He wouldn't leave him!"

"He'll be fine as long as we get him straight

to the vet!" Jo promised. "Boy, Drifter, are we glad to see you!"

Everything was blurred now – the people shouting and running, the first-aid, vehicles coming and going.

But there was time, after Nathan had been

driven away in the ambulance, for Krista to put her arms around Shining Star's neck, and for her to feel his shimmering cloud surround her one last time.

"I can't believe we did that!" she sighed.

"It's true," he assured her. For a moment he folded his wings around her.

She sighed. "And do you have to go now?"

The magical pony nodded.

"I'll miss you." She loved the softness of his white feathers, the silkiness of his mane. "Will I see you again?"

"Perhaps," he murmured. "But now I really must leave."

As Shining Star spread his wings once more, Krista saw the reason. It was her dad's car, driving fast along the wet sand. It screeched to a halt and her mum and dad leaped out.

"Are you OK?" Her mum sprinted towards Krista and Shining Star.

"Go!" Krista urged the flying pony.

"I'm fine!" she said to her mum. "Honestly, I'm totally fine!"

Out of the corner of her eye, Krista watched the wonderful pony trot off along the sand. She stood expecting the worst from her mum and dad. "Are you going to ground me again?" she asked unhappily.

"What you did was dangerous," her dad began. "You must promise *never* to do anything like it again."

But, guess what, her mum laughed, then hugged her and wouldn't stop.

"Krista, you never could stay still in one place for longer than five minutes!" her dad sighed.

"We heard all about what you did – you were a brave and amazing girl!" her mum said.

"Not me," Krista protested. "It was Star."

"Is that what you call him?" Krista's mum let her go so that the three of them could stand and watch the grey pony pick up speed and break into a canter along the beach.

But only Krista saw the magic silver cloud surrounding him. Only she saw him spread his wings and fly.

"He's quite a mystery," Krista's dad murmured, as Shining Star galloped out of sight.